I am an Aro Publishing Twenty Word Book

My twenty words are:

see	go (goes)
the	doesn't
farmer	care
tractor	bed
plows	dare
crops	it
stop (stops)	where
wants	steer
to	Oh
inside	dear

FUNNY FARM BOOKS

The Farmer's Tractor

Story by Wendy Kanno
Pictures by Bob Reese

ARO PUBLISHING

4

See the farmer's tractor.

The tractor

plows the crops.

See the farmer's tractor.

The tractor doesn't stop.

The farmer wants to go inside.

The tractor doesn't care.

The farmer

wants to go to bed.

The farmer

doesn't dare.

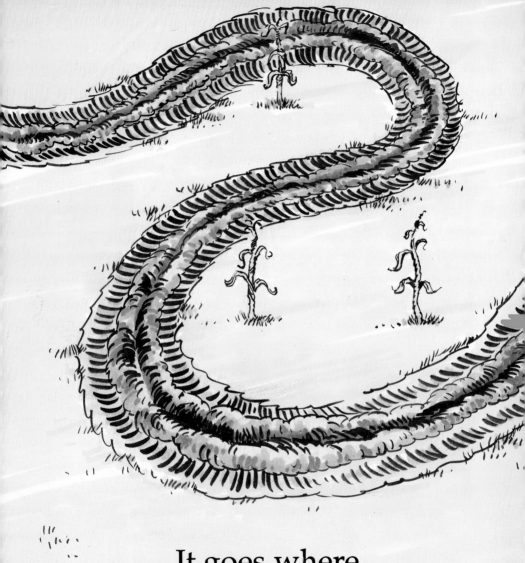

It goes where

it wants to.

The farmer doesn't steer!

It stops where it wants to.

Oh dear! Oh dear! Oh dear!